# The Boy with Glasses

Written by Stephanie Yang

Illustrated by Emilia Telios

Cover design and illustrations by Emilia Telios

Book Production by Miramare Ponte Press

Hardback ISBN-13:979-8-9852251-1-2

Paperback ISBN-13:979-8-9852251-0-5

eBook ISBN-13:979-8-9852251-2-9

Library of Congress Control Number: 2021922169

Yang, Stephanie

The Boy With Glasses / Stephanie Yang

When Teddy looks in the mirror, he only sees the awful things that the bullies call him. Unable to see his true reflection, Teddy goes through his days hiding from his image and wondering how to look normal, like everyone else. Will Teddy get to see his true reflection?

ISBN-(hc) 13:979-8-9852251-1-2

*I dedicate this story to my son, Emery.*
*May you always see how wonderfully made you are!*

Teddy looked at his reflection in a puddle,

but all he saw were four eyes.

Teddy looked at his reflection in the toy store window,

but all he saw was a glass face.

Teddy looked at his reflection in his bedroom mirror, but all he saw was a specky-nerd.

Now, Teddy wasn't any of the things the
bullies called him,
but the words made it hard for him to
see himself any other way.

Even though Teddy was friendly and welcoming,

the bullies called him "four eyes."

Even though Teddy was quick to share with his classmates,

the bullies called him "glass face."

Even though Teddy often cared for others,

the bullies called him "specky-nerd."

That's how it came to be that Teddy could no longer see
his true reflection.

"Why can't I just be normal like everyone else, Mama?"

Teddy cried out loud.

"Why am I so different?"

"You are the most handsome young man I know," his mama replied.

"Look, let me show you." Mama held up her special mirror.

"See? There's my kind, thoughtful, playful son."

But all Teddy could see was

a face full of specs.

The next morning was no different. Teddy passed his bedroom mirror.
"UGH!" he cried out in disgust, throwing his blanket over the mirror to
hide his reflection.

At school, Teddy hoped to avoid the bullies.

He crept from a bush to a wall to a trash can. But the bullies were nowhere to be found. Teddy was relieved—until something struck him:

If bullies weren't waiting around to pick on him,

then they must be bullying

someone else.

That's when Teddy saw her—the girl with glasses.

Today, she was the one being picked on.

"Four eyes!"

"Glass face!"

"Specky-nerd!"

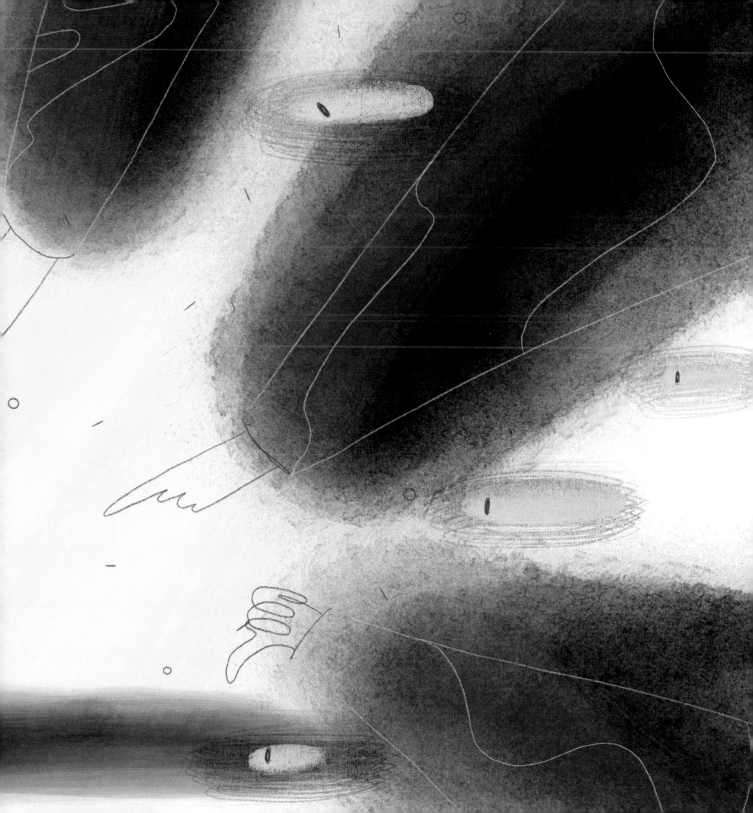

Teddy shook his head in confusion. He squinted to get a better look.

Nope, he couldn't understand why they called her such names.

All he saw was the most beautiful girl in the whole world.

Her glasses didn't make her a "glass face" or "four eyes."

They made her stand out; they made her unique—beautifully unique.

It started to rain. The bullies ran inside,

but the girl stood there alone, drenched in sadness.

Teddy noticed his own reflection in a growing puddle. It wasn't just any reflection, it was his true self. He didn't see a "four eyes," a "glass face," or a "specky-nerd" anymore. Yes, his glasses made him look a little different, but so did his long hair, his dark eyes, and his missing tooth. These things made him unique in his own special way! They made him *him*.

He felt his chest fill with the heat of new courage.

He marched right up to the girl with glasses and said, "You are not any of the things those bullies called you. You are you! You are unique in your own special way, and unique is beautiful."

She stood there quietly, her tears mixing with the puddle beneath her feet—the same puddle she was avoiding looking into.

"Look," said Teddy, pointing to her reflection. "I see you. I want you to see you too." The girl slowly glanced down to the puddle. She saw someone new!

Her true self smiled back at her. She noticed the second reflection in the puddle. It was unique too—warm and welcoming.

"My name is Grace," she said. "I see you, too."

# ABOUT THE AUTHOR

Stephanie Yang spent much of her life coping with bullying and trauma. Making up stories allowed her to escape to different worlds—the safe places away from hurtful words. Later in life, she became a mother to four wonderful children. Unfortunately, her babies grew up and experienced their own hardships. Stephanie wrote stories for them to help them cope with the hardships of their little lives. Stephanie later pursued an education in psychology. She wanted to not only help her own children but other children as well. Stephanie used beautiful pictures to help children cope with their own life struggles. Her hope is to use education, skill, and God's grace to continue to write children's books that will impact the lives of our little ones.

Made in the USA
Las Vegas, NV
10 November 2021